KEVIN VS THE UNICORNS

BY THE REMARKABLE DOUBLE ACT THAT IS

PHILIP REEVE AND SARAH MCINTYRE

OXFORD
UNIVERSITY PRESS

This is Kevin.

Kevin is a roly-poly flying pony.

In fact, Kevin is the one and only roly-poly flying pony. He doesn't mind too much, because he has his friends Max and Daisy to keep him company.

This is Max . . . and this is Daisy.

Kevin lives here, in a nest on
the roof of Max and Daisy's block
of flats in the town of Bumbleford. They
have lots of adventures together, and
lots of biscuits, and since adventures and
biscuits are Kevin's favourite things he's
mostly pretty happy. But sometimes—
just sometimes, when he's alone in his
nest and the wind is blowing from
the wild, wet hills of the Outermost
West—he feels a little bit sad, and wishes
there were some other roly-poly ponies
he could go flying with.

ONE

THE SNOOTY UNICORNS

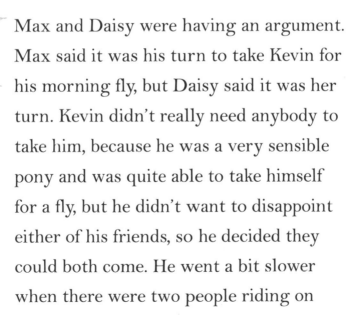

Max and Daisy were having an argument.
Max said it was his turn to take Kevin for
his morning fly, but Daisy said it was her
turn. Kevin didn't really need anybody to
take him, because he was a very sensible
pony and was quite able to take himself
for a fly, but he didn't want to disappoint
either of his friends, so he decided they
could both come. He went a bit slower
when there were two people riding on

him, but he didn't mind.

It was one of those mornings when the land and the sky had got all mixed up in the night. Sleepy clouds had settled on the hilltops for a snooze, and slithered down into the valleys, and got themselves all tangled in the branches of the trees. Kevin flew above them, with his shadow flitting over their white tops, and Max and Daisy looked down and saw the roofs and chimney pots of Bumbleford poking out of the mist below them.

Kevin flew towards the wild, wet hills of the Outermost West. He had lived in those hills once, until a big storm shook him out of his nest and blew him all the way to Bumbleford, where he met Max and Daisy. He couldn't see many of the hills

that morning, because the mist lay over
them like a thick, white quilt, but he could
see the spire of the church in the village of
Great Kerfuffle, which was on the edge of
the hills, and he headed towards that. Then
Max spotted something else poking out
of the mists just ahead. It was the top of
a round, green hill. A white marquee had
been pitched there, and next to it there was
a little cluster of people and ponies.

'Look!' said Max.

'Ponies!' said Kevin.

'Let's go down and say hello!' said Daisy.

When Kevin landed on the hilltop it turned out that the ponies weren't ponies at all. They were unicorns. Kevin nearly took off again, because he didn't like unicorns. They were always so pleased with themselves, prancing about in dappled glades with their fancy, glittery horns, or standing under rainbows, trying to look cool. But he had been wishing for some flying pony friends, and he supposed unicorns were probably the next best thing, so he decided to stay and find out what these unicorns were like.

They all looked very graceful and they

had rainbow-coloured manes and tails. On their backs sat girls wearing neat tweed jackets and big riding helmets. 'Oooh!' said all three girls when they saw Kevin touch down. 'A flying pony!'

'How common!' one of the unicorns sniffed.

'Look at his big round tummy!' said another.

'Look at his tiny little wings!'

'If the good Lord had meant us to fly he would have given us first-class airline tickets.'

'Humph,' said Kevin, deciding that he had been right about unicorns and wishing he had flown off again after all. But Max and Daisy were excited. They'd never met anyone else with a magical pony friend, and here was a whole bunch of them! They jumped down off Kevin's back and went over to meet the unicorns and their riders, while Kevin nibbled some grass and then wandered off towards the marquee. There was a folding table with tea things set up outside, and a tin from which an interesting biscuity smell was rising.

'What ho!' said the lady who seemed to be in charge of the riders. 'Flying pony, eh?

I've never seen one of those before. I'm Margery Flough. It's spelled F-L-O-U-G-H but it's pronounced "fluff". The girls here are Ethylwynne Brinsley Hey-ho, Lucie Ffarthingale-Ffitch, and Felicity Pemberton-Pemberton-Pemberton-Pemberton-Pemberton-Pemberton-Boggs. We're the WWHMPC.'

'The doubleyou-wubbleyou-what?' said Max.

'Wild Wet Hills Magical Pony Club. Do try to keep up! Say hello, girls!'

'Hmmmm,' said the girls, who didn't know what to make of their visitors.

'I'm Max,' said Max.

'And I'm Daisy,' said Daisy.

'What funny names!' said Ethylwynne Brinsley Hey-ho, wrinkling her nose.

'That's Kevin over there,' said Max, pointing to Kevin's large, white behind.

'We didn't know there was a Magical Pony Club . . .'

'Oh, yes,' said Margery Flough. 'We meet once a week here on Kerfuffle Hill, it's all jolly good fun.'

'Next Sunday we have our annual steeplechase race,' said Lucie Ffarthingale-Ffitch. 'I'm going to win this year on Moonshadow.' She patted her unicorn's mane, and the unicorn raised one eyebrow in a superior manner.

'The winner gets the Periwinkle Cup,' said Margery Flough. 'It's a jolly valuable trophy and a great honour.'

'The course is very difficult,' said

Ethylwynne Brinsley Hey-ho. 'We race all the way from here to the lake and back, and there are loads of jumps. And by the way, Lucie, my Twinklehooves can beat your Moonshadow any day.'

'Actually, my Rainbow Wind will beat both your unicorns, or my name isn't Felicity Pemberton-Pemberton-Pemberton-Pemberton-Pemberton-Pemberton-Boggs,' said Felicity Pemberton-Pemberton-Pemberton-Pemberton-Pemberton-Pemberton-Boggs.

Max and Daisy looked out into the mist. It was just starting to clear by then, and they could see the silver glimmer of a lake at the foot of the hill, and the steeplechase course leading down to it. Some of the jumps were made from old tractor tyres and stripy wooden poles. Others were disguised as giant horseshoes, or little buildings. Max and Daisy both knew Kevin could easily jump over those. Kevin could jump over full-sized buildings if he wanted to.

'Can Kevin be in the race?' Max asked.

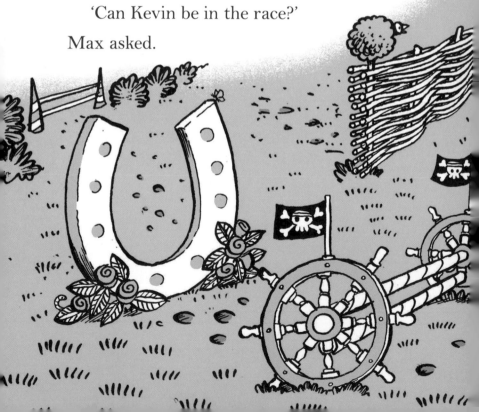

'Eww!' said the unicorn called Moonshadow.

'Hardly!' said Twinklehooves.

But Margery Flough said, 'What a jolly splendid idea! We could do with some new contestants to liven things up. We've never had a flying pony before. How long has he been in your family?'

'Since the big storm,' said Daisy.

'He crashed into our flat by accident and decided to stay,' explained Max. 'He lives in a nest on our roof.'

'Ewww!' said all the unicorns.

'You'll need the proper equipment,' said Ethylwynne.

'They haven't even got riding breeches, Mrs Flough,' said Twinklehooves.

'They haven't even got boots!' agreed

Lucie. 'Or hats, or anything!'

'And that pony doesn't look as if it's EVER had its tail plaited,' said Rainbow Wind.

Daisy felt cross. 'You're just a lot of snotty, snooty snobs!' she said.

Max agreed. 'Kevin's as good as your stupid unicorns any day!' he said. 'You'll see! We're going to win your silly race!'

The girls looked shocked, and so did their unicorns, but Margery Flough just laughed. She had been getting a bit worried about the WWHMPC. In the good old days, when she was a girl, there had been dozens

of unicorns and riders, but now there were only three. She thought it might be time to overlook a few of the club's strict rules and welcome in some new members, even if they didn't have the proper hats, and even if their magical pony was a bit on the roly-poly side. Anyway, she rather liked Max, Daisy, and Kevin.

'Jolly good show!' she said. 'That's the spirit! We'll see you and your flying chum on Sunday. Here's a form for your parents to fill out.' She reached into one of the pockets of her big tweedy coat and pulled out the form. Daisy took it.

'See you on Sunday,' Max said, and went to fetch Kevin.

Kevin had knocked over the tin with the interesting smell and its lid had come off and a lot of very interesting biscuits had rolled out. When Max told him they were going to be in a race he stopped snuffling them up just long enough to say, 'What race?'

'The Wild Wet Hills Magical Pony Club Steeplechase Race,' said Max. 'If you win, you get the Periwinkle Cup.'

'Oh,' said Kevin. 'Can you eat it?'

'I don't think so.'

'Will they have more biscuits? Because these were very nice biscuits, only there weren't enough of them.'

'I expect so,' said Max.

'OK' said Kevin. 'Let's do it!'

Max and Daisy climbed on his back and they flew home to Bumbleford, wondering what they had let themselves in for.

TWO
TIFFANY BINNS TAKES CHARGE

Max was a bit worried about what Mum
and Dad would say when he told them he
had signed Kevin up for a steeplechase.
But when he showed them the form and
told them about the magical pony club
they didn't mind at all. 'That's nice!' said
Dad. 'New friends for you and Kevin.'

Max and Daisy looked at each other,
but they didn't say anything. They didn't

think those snooty unicorns and their snooty riders would turn out to be friends, exactly.

'You should talk to Tiffany,' said Mum. 'I think she used to be in that pony club. She'll know all about their steeplechase.'

Tiffany Binns lived in the flat below. After tea, Max, Daisy, and Kevin all squeezed into the lift and went down to visit her. Tiffany was a fluttery, twittery sort of person but she was very friendly and Max, Daisy, and Kevin liked her. They liked visiting her flat, too, because it was laid out exactly the same as the flat they lived in, with the hallway and kitchen and

living room and bedrooms all in the same place, but all the stuff was different, so it was like stepping into a parallel universe. It smelled nice too, because Tiffany's hobby was baking. That day, as if she had known that Kevin would be calling, she had been baking biscuits. 'You're just in time to test them for me,' she said, letting her visitors in.

'These,' said Kevin after a few minutes, 'are Very Good Biscuits.'

'We're going to enter Kevin for the Wild Wet Hills Magical Pony Club Steeplechase,' said Max.

'Mum said you'd know all about it,' said Daisy.

Tiffany shuddered. 'The Wild Wet Hills Magical Pony Club? It's a long time since I heard that name . . .'

'Is it true you used to be a member?' asked Max.

Tiffany went and fetched an old shoe box from the cupboard in her hallway. When she took the lid off it turned out to be full of faded old rosettes and photos. She held up one of the photos. It showed her as a girl, sitting on the back of a slightly

peculiar-looking unicorn. 'This is a picture
of me and Bramble,' she said. 'Bramble is the
one underneath. He was my pony when I was
your age. I used to live in Slight Kerfuffle,
which is just up the road from Great Kerfuffle.
I rode Bramble everywhere.'

'And you were in the Magical Pony Club!' said Daisy, spotting a rosette with the WWHMPC logo in the box. 'Did you ride Bramble in their steeplechase?'

'Oh yes,' said Tiffany.

'Did you win?' Max wondered.

'No, I didn't,' said Tiffany sadly. 'Those pony club girls were mean. They were horrid to me because I didn't have all the right gear, and their unicorns were horrible to Bramble because he wasn't a thoroughbred pedigree unicorn like them—his mum was a donkey, you see. And they made absolutely sure we didn't win their stupid steeplechase.' She shuddered again. 'Pansy Ffarthingale-Ffitch, she was the worst of them.'

'There's a Lucie Ffarthingale-Ffitch in the club now,' said Daisy.

'That must be Pansy's daughter,' said Tiffany. 'Those Ffarthingale-Ffitches will go to any lengths to win the steeplechase. They take home the Periwinkle Cup every year. I'd love to see someone beat them for once.'

'Kevin will!' said Max. 'Kevin can fly—those stuck-up unicorns will never be able to keep up with him!'

Tiffany looked thoughtful for a moment. Then she shook her head. 'It's no use. You see, it's not just about the race. To even enter you have to make sure your pony is properly groomed and has its mane and tail plaited just right.'

'That's why we came to see you!' said Daisy. 'So you can tell us what to do!'

'My pony club days are long behind me,' said Tiffany, shaking her head again as she put the lid back on her box of mementoes. 'The last time I took part in their steeplechase, Pansy Ffarthingale-Ffitch and her friends played all sorts of beastly tricks to stop us winning. We were both so embarrassed we vowed we'd never race again.'

'But you could help us win!' said Max. 'You could be our trainer!'

Tiffany blinked at them. 'Well,' she said. 'I suppose I could . . . You'd have to agree to do everything I tell you.'

'Of course!' said Max, Kevin, and Daisy.

'How do we start?' asked Max.

'First,' said Tiffany, 'No More Biscuits.'

She swiped the plate of home-baked biscuits out from under Kevin's nose just as he leaned in for third helpings. Kevin gasped. 'I don't know if you've noticed,' said Tiffany, 'but Kevin is a little, tiny bit on the plump side.'

'He's meant to be!' said Daisy.

'He's a roly-poly flying pony,' said Max.

'That's the best sort,' said Kevin.

'If he's entering the steeplechase he needs to have a healthy diet,' said Tiffany. 'And plenty of exercise. You must take him for at least a five-mile flap every day. And no more riding up and down in the lift— use the stairs, it'll be much better for you.'

Kevin was starting to think that maybe winning the Periwinkle Cup wasn't worth the effort after all, but Max said, 'Don't worry, Kevin, it's only for a few days, and when we've won, we'll get you LOADS of biscuits.'

'Enough to fill the Periwinkle Cup!' Daisy promised.

Kevin thought about it. 'Is it a big sort of cup?' he asked.

'Oh it's huge,' said Tiffany. 'And it's made of solid gold!'

Kevin didn't really care too much what it was made of, he was more interested in how many biscuits you could fit in it. Quite a lot, by the sound of it. He remembered how rude those unicorns had been, and imagined how nice it would be to beat them.

'Well, all right,' he said.

THREE

KEVIN IN TRAINING

And so training began. Every morning Max and Kevin went for a long fly over Bumbleford, all the way to the beach at Farsight Cove. Daisy and Tiffany would drive down in Tiffany's car to meet them there, and Kevin would practise galloping along the sand and flapping over big rocks, while Tiffany rode alongside on her bicycle shouting encouraging things at them through a megaphone.

When they got home again, instead of flying to his nest on the roof, Kevin would land on the pavement outside the building and clip-clop all the way up the stairs. By the end of the week he was still the same shape, because that is the shape that roly-poly flying ponies are meant to be, and he was having a lot of dreams about biscuits, but he was feeling much fitter, and ready to face the unicorns. Gordon from Flat

3 kept his racing pigeons in a coop on the roof, and they gave Kevin all sorts of useful tips about winning races.

Of course it wasn't just Kevin who
needed to prepare. Max was in training
too. He was going to be the one riding
Kevin during the big race, because he
was smaller and lighter than Daisy, and
Tiffany said that every kilo counted.
She was making sure Max would have
the proper things to wear, too. Max had
never bothered with special riding clothes
before, but Tiffany gave him her old riding
jacket, and Mrs Brown in Flat 1 got
out her sewing machine and altered

it to fit him. Tiffany also lent him her riding helmet, but her boots were too small for him, so he had to wear his wellie boots instead.

Very early on the day of the race, Max put on his outfit, and Mum, and Dad, and Tiffany, and all the neighbours gathered on the roof to watch while Max and Daisy carefully brushed and combed Kevin until he was as smooth and shiny as a smooth and shiny thing. They polished his hooves, and tied ribbons into his mane, and Daisy did his tail in a fat French plait. When they showed him his reflection in a mirror Kevin thought he looked a bit of a twit, and Max in his riding helmet and jacket and wellies felt silly too, but Tiffany said they were both Just Right.

Then Max jumped onto Kevin's back and they took off and flew away, while everybody on the roof cheered and then went running downstairs to pile into Mum's car and the Browns' new camper van, and follow them along the winding roads which led towards the wild, wet hills. Handwritten signs pinned to fence

posts pointed the way. Up on Kerfuffle
Hill, brightly coloured bunting was
dancing in the breeze and some ladies had
set up a stall selling tea and cakes. But it

didn't look as if many people had turned up to watch the steeplechase: the only other people on the hilltop were the pony club girls with their unicorns, some of their mums and dads, and a centaur called Cedric. Max and Kevin knew Cedric quite well, and they could tell from the scowl on his usually cheerful face that he was in a bad mood.

'This is rubbish,' said Cedric, when
Kevin landed beside him. 'I heard about this
steeplechase and thought I'd have a go, but
those unicorns say I can't join in unless I've
got a rider. I told them I was half pony and
half person so I was my own rider, but they
said that's against the rules. I'm off.'

'You could stay and watch . . .' said Max.
But Cedric was already cantering away.

Margery Flough came bustling over.
'I'm sorry about your centaur chum,'
she said.

'But there's only so far I can bend the rules. Perhaps he can come back with a rider next year. But at least you're here! I'm jolly glad you've decided to enter. Should shake things up a bit, what?' She ticked off Max and Kevin's names on her clipboard.

The other girls rode over, not looking nearly so pleased to see Kevin and Max.

'Those aren't real riding boots!' said Felicity Pemberton-Pemberton-Pemberton-Pemberton-Pemberton-Pemberton-Boggs.

'That hat is awfully unfashionable,' said Ethylwynne Brinsley Hey-ho.

The unicorns looked Kevin up and down. Rainbow Wind gave him a quick sniff and pulled back hastily. 'Ewww! You smell like a pony! Aren't you wearing any

perfume? I am wearing Eau de Paddock.'

'Your hooves haven't been painted,' said Twinklehooves. 'Personally I wouldn't be seen dead without nicely painted hooves.'

'Is your tail supposed to be plaited?' sneered Moonshadow. 'It looks like a soggy pretzel.'

'And I hope you don't think you're going to fly round the course,' said Lucie Ffarthingale-Ffitch. She turned to her mum, who looked exactly like a larger version of her. 'Mummy, tell him flying's not allowed!'

'Of course, dear,' said her mother. 'The rules don't say anything about people being allowed to FLY over the jumps.'

'But they don't say anything about people NOT being allowed to fly over the jumps,' said Tiffany Binns, arriving just then with Daisy, Mum and Dad, Gordon, and the Browns. 'Goodness gracious!' said Mrs Ffarthingale-Ffitch. 'It's Tiffany Binns! Girls, this is Tiffany, she used to be in the club when I was your age. We all used to call her "Rubbish Binns" because her name is Binns and she was a bit rubbish, hahaha! How are you these days, Rubbish? Whatever was the name of that strange little unicorn you used to go about on—Bumble? Burble?'

'Bramble,' said Tiffany, glaring at her.

'Bramble, that was it! I wonder whatever happened to him?'

'He was so upset at the way you lot treated him that he ran away and vowed never to take part in a race ever again,' said Tiffany, crossly. 'Poor Bramble! He should have won that last steeplechase! We trained for weeks!'

'But he came in last!' said Mrs Ffarthingale-Ffitch.

'Only because you set up a fake diversion that added ten miles to the course,' said Tiffany.

'And he didn't clear the final jump!'

'Only because you raised it sixty centimetres while nobody was looking!'

'And he wasn't properly groomed—his hair was sticking out in all directions, he looked like a dandelion clock!'

'Only because you secretly hid a giant Van der Graaff static electricity generator behind a bush and turned it

on when he trotted past!' shouted Tiffany.
'You're a rotten cheat, Pansy Ffarthingale-
Ffitch, and I'm here to make sure that
your rotten daughter doesn't cheat like
you did!'

'Oh!' said Lucie, turning pink, red, and
finally purple with anger.

But her mother simply smiled at
Tiffany Binns and said, 'I agree.'

'You do?' said Tiffany.

'Oh, absolutely. We mustn't have any cheating. For instance, if any riders were to get their ponies to fly over the jumps that would definitely be cheating, wouldn't it, Mrs Flough?'

'Well . . .' said Margery Flough, who had been busily looking through the WWHMPC rule book, but hadn't found anything about flying ponies.

'It would give them a completely unfair advantage,' agreed Ethylwynne Brinsley Hey-ho's mum.

'Wouldn't be in the spirit of the competition at all,' said Felicity Pemberton-Pemberton-Pemberton-Pemberton-Pemberton-Pemberton-Boggs's dad. His name was Pemberton Pemberton-Pemberton-

Pemberton-Pemberton-Pemberton
-Pemberton-Boggs and he was the owner of
the biggest house in Great Kerfuffle, and a
very important person.

'Well I suppose it would be a little unfair,'
said Margery Flough, realizing that she was
outnumbered.

'But Kevin can't gallop all the way,'
wailed Max. 'His legs are only little!'

'And whose fault is that?' sniffed Lucie

Ffarthingale-Ffitch.

'I tell you what,' said Margery Flough, because she really did want Kevin to be in the race, 'as it's Kevin's first time and he only has little legs, we'll give him a thirty-second head start, how does that sound?'

It didn't sound very good to anybody— the pony club girls didn't see why Kevin should get special treatment, and Max

and Daisy knew that a thirty-second head
start or even a thirty-minute head start
wasn't going to help Kevin win against
those strong, sleek, long-legged unicorns.
But Margery Flough said she was Club
President and her decision was final, so
everyone moved over to the starting line.
There was a big metal box there, sealed
with chains and padlocks.

'In this box,' said
Margery Flough, 'is
the famous and valuable
Periwinkle Cup. When
the race is over, it will be
presented to the winner. We were hoping
to get local pop sensation Misty Twiglet
to do the presentation, but she's away
in Dublin, recording an album with the

famous Irish songstress Lána Bus. Luckily for us, the Mayor of Bumbleford has agreed to do the presenting instead.'

'And may the best pony win!' said the Mayor. She looked a bit different from the last time Max had seen her—he didn't remember her having that moustache before— but he supposed that if a mayor wanted to grow a moustache it was her own business. Anyway, he and Kevin had more important things to think about. The race was about to start!

FOUR
THE GREAT RACE

Margery Flough fired her starting pistol, and they were off! Well, Kevin was. He kept his wings neatly folded, but his little legs were a blur as he went galloping along the first part of the course. 'Ke-vin! Ke-vin! Ke-vin,' chanted Daisy and all Kevin's other friends. Bouncing along on his back, Max couldn't believe how fast his roly-poly friend was running. Perhaps there was a chance they might win after all!

Then, thirty seconds later, Margery Flough fired the pistol again, and about three seconds after that a white blur went past on Kevin's left, and a pale-pink blur went past on his right, and a sky-blue blur zoomed straight overhead, landed in front of him, and galloped off, splattering mud in his face. Those unicorns moved

so fast that it made Kevin feel as if he
was standing still, even though he was
galloping as fast as he could gallop.

   The unicorns arrived at the first jump.
It was a sort of tall hedge, and all three
unicorns sailed straight over it, with Lucie
Ffarthingale-Ffitch on Moonshadow in
the lead. When Kevin came panting up
to the hedge he did his best to jump it,
he really did, but it all went wrong and
he landed flump on the top and had to
wriggle off. On the far side of the hedge

there was a deep, squidgy pool of mud, and he fell into it with a splat. 'Who put a deep, squidgy pool of mud here?' shouted Max, as they scrambled ashore. But there was no one to hear him—the unicorns were far ahead of them, leaping easily over jump after jump.

Kevin shook off as much mud as he could and galloped towards the second jump, which was built to look like a little castle. He didn't gallop very fast though, because he was getting tired, and his hooves ached, and although he was usually a cheerful, optimistic sort of pony, he was starting to think he had no hope at all of winning the race.

About halfway to the jump he was overtaken by two more competitors. Neville and Beyoncé were the most adventurous guinea pigs in all of Bumbleford, and when they heard about the steeplechase they had decided to escape from their hutch and win the Periwinkle Cup for themselves. They hadn't been able to agree on who should be the pony and who should be the rider so they kept having to stop and swap places, but they were still faster than Kevin. When he saw them go by, Kevin went even slower. And when he was overtaken by a snail with a small frog riding on its shell, he came to a complete stop, about two metres from the castle-shaped jump.

'This is pointless,' said Kevin.

'Only because they won't let you fly,' said Max.

'Mmmmff!' said the castle-shaped jump.

Max looked hard at the jump. 'That pretend castle just said "Mmmmff!"' he said.

'Yes, I heard it,' agreed Kevin.

'That's a bit odd, isn't it?' asked Max.

Kevin shrugged. He didn't know what pretend castles usually said.

Max went over to the jump and knocked on its little door. 'Mmmff mmmff!' said the voice from inside. Max opened the

MMMMMMF!

door. Inside the jump there was a person.
The person had been tied up and gagged.
'Mmmmff!' they said.

Kevin got his nose under one end of
the jump and pushed. Max grabbed the
other end and heaved, and together they
managed to topple the jump over so they
could see who the person underneath was.
It took Max a moment to recognize her
without her official hat, robes, and chain
of office, but when he undid the gag that

someone had tied around her face he could see who she was.

'Gasp!' he gasped. 'You're the Mayor of Bumbleford! But you're up at the finishing line, getting ready to award the prize!'

'To a stupid unicorn,' grumbled Kevin.

'We saw you there!' said Max.

'That wasn't me!' the Mayor explained. 'I was on my way here when someone jumped out from behind a bush, stole my

mayoral regalia, and left me tied up under this jump.'

'Who would do such a thing?' gasped Max.

But Kevin was already thinking back to the fake mayor they'd seen earlier with Margery Flough. He had thought at the time there was something oddly familiar about that mayor's moustache, and now it suddenly made sense.

'It was BAZ GUMPTION!' he said.

And he was right.

Baz Gumption was Bumbleford's very own Criminal Mastermind. He had caused a lot of trouble for Kevin and Max that time he tried stealing all the town's biscuits. Thanks to them, he had been arrested and sent to prison, but because of an administrative error he had ended up in Horse Prison, where some of the naughtiest horses in the country were locked up. There, Baz had made friends with a bad unicorn called Pointy Steve, who had told him about the Wild Wet Hills Magical Pony Club. When Baz heard about the ancient and valuable Periwinkle Cup he was so excited that he broke out of prison that very afternoon. 'I'll melt that cup down and live like a king on all the gold!'

he had chortled, as he hid himself inside
a big pile of horse poo and old straw that
was being removed from the prison.

A faint smell of straw and horse poo
still clung to him as he waited at the finish
line of the steeplechase, but most of the
people involved with the WWHMPC
smelled a bit like that, so nobody noticed.
Anyway, everyone was far too busy

watching the racecourse to see which unicorn would come galloping up to the finish line first.

'Ke-vin! Ke-vin!' Daisy was still chanting, but she wasn't feeling very hopeful. And sure enough, when the racers came into view, there was no sign of Max and Kevin. Ethylwynne Brinsley Hey-ho on Twinklehooves was in third place, mainly because someone had a rigged a tripwire which tangled Twinklehooves's legs and

made him face-plant in the water jump, wasting valuable time. Felicity Pemberton- Pemberton-Pemberton-Pemberton- Pemberton-Pemberton-Boggs on Rainbow Wind was second, mostly because someone had left loads of muffins all over the final jump and Rainbow Wind just could not resist a muffin.

And Lucie Ffarthingale- Ffitch was in the lead, because she

had rigged the tripwire
and placed the muffins to make sure she
and Moonshadow came first.

'And Moonshadow wins it by a horn!'
cried Margery Flough, as Moonshadow
crossed the line. The other unicorns were
just behind him, and they all drew up
expectantly in front of the prize-giving
stand where the Mayor was waiting. A

few minutes later, Neville and
Beyoncé crossed the line too,
and a little while after that,
a snail with a frog on its back
appeared—but there was no
sign of Max and Kevin.

'Whatever's happened
to them?' asked Daisy.

'I'm sure they'll straggle
in eventually,' said Margery
Flough. 'But we can't
waste time waiting for
slowcoaches. The Mayor is
a very busy woman, we
must let her get on with the

prize awarding.'

'Thank you!' said the mayor, whose voice had turned surprisingly deep. 'Ladies and gentlemen, boys and girls, ponies, unicorns, and random woodland creatures, it gives me great pleasure to present the prizes for this, the one thousand, three hundred and sixty-second WWHMPC steeplechase. In third place we have Ethylwynne Brinsley Hey-ho on Twinklehooves . . .' The mayor passed a blue rosette to Ethylwynne. 'In second place, Felicity Pemberton-Pemberton-Pemberton-Pemberton-Pemberton-Boggs . . .'

'It's Pemberton-Pemberton-Pemberton-Pemberton-Pemberton-PEMBERTON-Boggs, actually,' shouted Felicity's dad.

The Mayor ignored him, and shoved

a red 2nd Place rosette into Felicity's
hands. 'But what we've all been waiting
for,' she said gruffly, 'is the magnificent
First Prize—the ancient and valuable
Periwinkle Cup!'

Margery Flough undid the padlocks
and chains on the box and took out the

trophy. It was a huge, jewelled cup, and it shone golden in the sunshine. It was the sort of cup that ought to be accompanied by the eerie singing of angelic choirs, Daisy thought. And for a moment, as she stood shielding her eyes against its brightness, she thought she COULD hear eerie singing.

But it wasn't an angelic choir.

It was Kevin and Max. Kevin was flying towards the finish line as fast as his muddy wings could carry him, and he and Max were both yelling, 'NOOOOO!'

'Well, really,' said Lucie Ffarthingale-Ffitch. 'How vulgar!'

'Don't let—that's not the real mayor—it's BAZ GUMPTION!' shouted Max, as Kevin landed.

'Please be quiet,' said Margery Flough, sternly. 'We have reached the most important moment of the prize-giving. Whatever you have to say can wait until afterwards, I'm sure.'

'But—' said Max.

'Thank you, Mrs Flough,' said the Mayor, glaring at Max and Kevin. 'I am pleased to announce that this year the Periwinkle Cup will be awarded to . . . ME!'

'Eh?' gasped Lucie Ffarthingale-Ffitch, who was already reaching out to grab the cup.

'That's right!' cackled the Mayor, ripping off her hat and wig to reveal that she really was Baz Gumption, just as Max had said. 'Why should a magnificent antique like this be used as a prize by your stupid pony club when it could be melted down to buy posh

stuff for me? So long, suckers!'

'Quick!' shouted Daisy. 'Get him!'

But as everyone surged towards the
podium there came a great rumbling of
hooves and from out of the trees behind
the tea tent galloped a huge, tough-looking
unicorn. Sunlight flashed from his horn as
he charged across the hilltop, with people
jumping out of his way as he came. As he
passed the podium, Baz Gumption leaped

onto his back. 'Hi-ho, Pointy Steve!' Baz shouted, waving the Periwinkle Cup while the unicorn reared up and pummelled the air with its front hooves. Then it galloped away, and Baz's triumphant laughter faded into the distance.

'Told you so,' said Max.

'Don't just stand there!' shrieked Margery Flough. 'Follow that unicorn!'

Lucie, Ethylwynne, and Felicity all urged their unicorns after the speeding villains, but the unicorns were tired out after the steeplechase and it didn't look as if they would be able to catch up with Pointy Steve.

'We'll stop him!' said Daisy. She scrambled up onto Kevin's back behind Max, and Kevin flapped his wings so hard that all the onlookers were speckled with mud as he zoomed up into the sky.

While everyone was busy watching the chase, or calling the police on their mobile phones, Neville and Beyoncé clambered onto the winners' podium and proudly helped themselves to the 1st Place rosette. (There were no rosettes left for the frog

and the snail, but they didn't care—they
thought it was the taking
part that counted.)

FIVE

THE CHASE TO THE EDGE OF THE WORLD

Pointy Steve raced across the wild, wet hills, and Moonshadow, Rainbow Wind, and Twinklehooves were close behind. The thunder of their hooves echoed from the hillsides. Families of fauns and other magical creatures peered from the woods as the unicorns sped by, flocks of frightened fairies flapped out of the way, and a pixie was so surprised he fell off his toadstool.

Baz Gumption clung to
Pointy Steve's mane with one
hand and clutched the Periwinkle
Cup in the other. He looked back and
saw the other unicorns gaining on him,
but his triumphant grin did not fade. He
had been expecting the pony club to
chase him. He let go of Pointy Steve's
mane for just long enough to press
a button on a remote control in his
pocket. A smoke canister he had
taped to Pointy Steve's bottom
let out a thick cloud of
black smoke.

The smoke engulfed
Moonshadow, Twinklehooves,
and Rainbow Wind. Not only
could they not see Pointy Steve
any more, they couldn't see
where they were going!

DOOF! Twinklehooves crashed
into a tree.

'I can't see a bally thing!' wailed
Felicity.

But a voice from somewhere
above her yelled, 'We can!'

It was Kevin, with Max and Daisy on
his back, soaring high above the smoke
cloud. They could see Pointy Steve
pounding over a windswept hilltop, zig-
zagging between ancient burial mounds,
whose ghosts came flapping out like

excitable laundry to see what all the
fuss was about. Kevin zoomed after him.
Max and Daisy clung on tight while
the rushing wind restyled their hair.

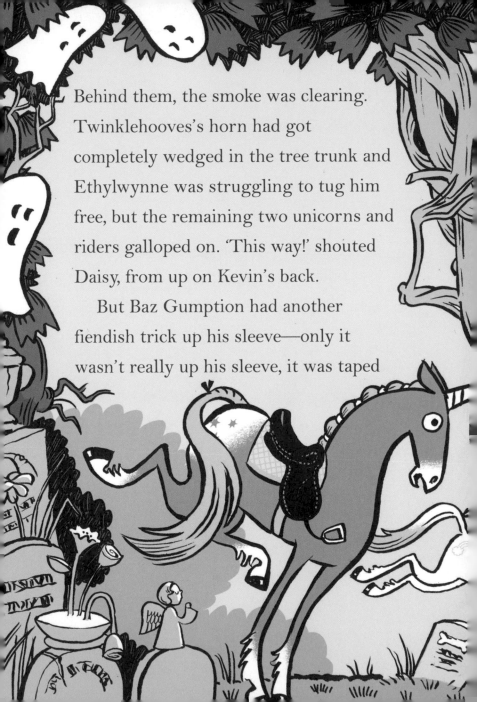

Behind them, the smoke was clearing. Twinklehooves's horn had got completely wedged in the tree trunk and Ethylwynne was struggling to tug him free, but the remaining two unicorns and riders galloped on. 'This way!' shouted Daisy, from up on Kevin's back.

But Baz Gumption had another fiendish trick up his sleeve—only it wasn't really up his sleeve, it was taped

to the other side of Pointy
Steve's bottom. It was a
canister full of slippery soap,
and when Baz pressed a second
button on his remote control the soap
squirted all over the ground behind
him. Moonshadow spotted the slick
just in time and jumped over it, but
Rainbow Wind galloped into it,
lost her footing, and tumbled
with a SPLAT into a bog
beside the road.

Felicity flew off her back and landed head-first in the mud.

Pointy Steve went racing on. He had been training every day while he was in Horse Prison, but even so, he was starting to tire. Kevin was keeping up with him easily now, and Moonshadow was gaining again.

'You can't get away, Baz Gumption!' shouted Max. 'Give us the cup!'

'Not on your nelly!' Baz yelled back.

Pointy Steve galloped over another hill. There ahead stood a lorry, parked in the middle of nowhere, with its back door open, and a ramp leading up into it. Pointy Steve clattered up the ramp into the lorry, and Baz scrambled off his back and into the driver's seat. The lorry roared off at top speed.

'He won't get far!' said Daisy. 'Look! There's the sea!'

It was true. Pointy Steve had galloped so far, so fast, that they were almost at the edge of the wild, wet hills. Just ahead of them the land came to a sudden end in dark cliffs, jagged rocks, and the tumbling white surf of the western sea. Baz's lorry was speeding straight towards a cliff!

'Baz! Stop!' shouted Max. 'You'll crash over!'

'You'll damage the Periwinkle Cup!' screeched Lucie. Moonshadow put on a last burst of speed and she leaned forward over his streaming mane, reaching for a handhold on the back of the lorry. 'Stop!' she shouted. But Baz paid no attention. The lorry went bucketing over the

100

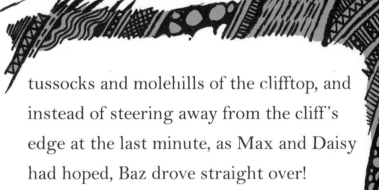

tussocks and molehills of the clifftop, and instead of steering away from the cliff's edge at the last minute, as Max and Daisy had hoped, Baz drove straight over!

They soon saw why. Just as the lorry began to fall, Baz pulled a lever on the dashboard and two powerful helicopter rotors sprang out of its sides. With a roar of whirling blades the lorry soared upwards and flew off across the sea.

Moonshadow, galloping flat out across the clifftop, stopped just in time at the very edge of the drop. But Lucie Ffarthingale-Ffitch kept going, hurtling

over her unicorn's head and out over the
edge of the cliff. 'Aiiieeeee!' she said, as
she started to plummet towards the sharp
black rocks below. 'Oooof!' she added, as
she landed on a dead tree which grew out

of the cliff face about ten metres down. She clung there, staring down at the cold white waves which prowled and snarled among the rocks beneath her. A crowd of Sea Monkeys came spilling out of their homes in the caves at the cliff's foot to watch the fun and make rude faces at her.

Kevin had been flying after the lorry, but when Max looked back and saw Lucie's predicament he knew they had to help. 'Turn around!' he told Kevin.

'But Lucie's horrid,' Daisy reminded him.

'We still can't let her fall,' Max said.

'She isn't falling,' Daisy pointed out. 'She's perfectly safe on that handy tree.'

'Creak, crunch, plink!' said the handy tree, as its dry old roots pulled free of the

cliff face one by one.
(It was a very old
tree and had never
been meant
to bear the
weight of a whole
Ffarthingale-Ffitch).

'Help!' shouted
Lucie.

'Please do
something!' wailed
Moonshadow,
cantering frantically
to and fro along the
clifftop.

'This,' said Kevin,
'is a job for a roly-
poly flying pony.'

And he did a swoopy sort of U-turn in mid-air and flew down to grab Lucie by the back of her jodhpurs, just as the tree tore free of the cliff face and went tumbling down, down, down to smash upon the rocks far below.

'Booo!' said the Sea Monkeys, who thought it would have been much funnier to let Lucie fall.

'Phew!' said Lucie. 'That was really brave. I'm sorry I was rude about your weird pony now.'

'You were pretty brave yourself,' admitted Max.

'Yes,' said Daisy, 'you nearly caught up with that lorry.'

'I didn't though,' said Lucie sadly. 'Baz Gumption got clean away with the cup.'

They all stood and looked out over the clifftop. Baz's lorry was so far away that it looked no bigger than a matchbox, and they could hardly hear the sound of its engines.

'Where do you think he's going?' asked Max.

'Islands,' said Kevin. He didn't remember ever having been to this part of the wild, wet hills before but somehow he knew that there were islands, just out of sight over there in the haze where the sea met the sky. 'There are islands,' he said.

'I bet Baz has a secret hideout on one of them,' said Daisy.

'Quick!' said Max, 'let's fly after him and find out where it is! Lucie, can you ride back to Great Kerfuffle and tell the police what's happened?'

Lucie hesitated for a moment, because she thought she was the most important person in this story and she ought to be the one following Baz Gumption to the islands. But Moonshadow couldn't fly, and unicorns are rubbish at swimming because they hate getting their manes wet, so she had to admit that following Baz was Kevin's job, not hers.

'All right,' she said, and then, a bit
grumpily, 'Good luck!'

So Kevin flapped into the air again and
set off across the sea, following the tiny,
dwindling speck that was Baz Gumption's
flying lorry.

SIX

THE ISLANDS

There were loads of islands in the western sea, but most of them weren't the sort of islands you can find on a map. These were magical islands, and they came and went like shadows, so people had given up on trying to make maps of them and decided that they had never existed at all. But there they were—or sometimes weren't— and on their sandy beaches and green hills lived all sorts of strange creatures.

As Kevin, Max, and Daisy flew over the
sea they passed islands full of mermaids,
islands full of trolls, and islands where
enormous, sleepy sea-serpents basked
lazily in the afternoon sun. But they
saw no sign of Baz Gumption or
Pointy Steve, and before long Kevin's
wings started to get tired. They
were only little wings, and they had
flown a long way that day.

At last, the highest of all the
islands rose ahead. It had steep
mountains in the middle of it,

and on the sides of the mountains
were meadows of lush, green,
wind-blown grass, speckled
with wild flowers. Kevin
thought that grass looked
Very Tasty. 'Lunchtime,' he
said firmly, and fluttered
down to land in one of
the meadows.

He had been right
about the grass—it
was Very Tasty
Indeed.

But Max and Daisy were hungry too, and grass was no use to them, however tasty it was. 'We should have brought packed lunches,' said Daisy. But of course, when they left home that morning, they hadn't expected to be flying to unknown islands in the western sea.

Max walked over to the edge of the meadow, hoping to see some apples or berries he could pick. Instead, he saw Baz Gumption. The ground fell away steeply at the meadow's edge and far down below, on a flat space beside the island's shore, the flying lorry was parked.

Pointy Steve was standing beside it, and Baz Gumption was fiddling about with something on the seashore.

'What are they doing here?' asked Daisy, when Max called her over to look.

'Maybe the lorry ran out of petrol,' said Max.

'Maybe they stopped for a wee,' mused Daisy.

'Maybe they stopped for a biscuit,' suggested Kevin, trotting over to see what Max and Daisy were talking about. He had enjoyed the grass, but he wished he had something a bit more sort of biscuity for dessert. (He was out of luck though—this wasn't a dessert island.)

'Look!' said Max. 'There's the Periwinkle Cup, sticking out of that bag! If we swooped down we could grab it.'

'But Baz and Pointy Steve will see us coming!' said Daisy.

'So what?' said Max. 'There's three of us and only two of them.'

Kevin was a bit nervous. Pointy Steve looked big and tough and more than a match for a flying pony, even a roly-poly one. Not only that, he wasn't sure that he liked this island. Ever since he landed here he kept getting the feeling that somebody was watching him. 'What if Baz Gumption has friends here?' he said.

Max and Daisy looked around at the woods and hills. They couldn't see anyone. 'Max is right,' said Daisy. 'We should grab the cup now, before they finish refuelling their lorry or doing wees or whatever it is they stopped here for.'

'All right,' said Kevin, and Max and
Daisy climbed onto his back. He took a
quick run-up, leaped off the hillside, and
went gliding down towards the parked
lorry with the wind ruffling his wing-
feathers. Daisy held onto the back of Max's
trousers, and Max leaned down, reaching
out a hand to grab the open bag
in which they could all see the
Periwinkle Cup gleaming.

But just as they were nearly on top of it, disaster struck. Max's riding helmet, which was really Tiffany Binns's riding helmet and a little bit too big for Max, dropped off his head. It landed with a loud bonk on the ground beside Pointy Steve, and rolled down onto the beach.

Pointy Steve looked around, and saw the helmet rolling by. He looked up, and saw Kevin zooming past. He guessed at once what Kevin was zooming for, and quickly galloped ahead

of him, hooking the
bag's handles
on his horn.
'Oh no you don't!'
growled Pointy Steve.
Baz Gumption
heard the commotion
and came running from
the beach. 'What's going on?'
'We've come to get
the Periwinkle Cup!'
said Daisy.

'You have to give it back!' said Max.

'You are a Bad Man,' said Kevin, who felt he ought to say something. He landed in front of Pointy Steve, and regretted it, because Pointy Steve really was a very big unicorn, and that horn looked really pointy.

Baz Gumption laughed the laugh of a proper villain: 'MwaAA-HaHaHaHa!' it went.

Pointy Steve laughed the laugh of a bad unicorn: 'Eeee-EE-EE-eeee!' (It was more of a neigh than a laugh, to be fair.)

'What's so funny?' asked Daisy.

'You think you can foil my brilliant scheme!' chuckled Baz. 'That's the funniest thing I've ever heard! You kids are priceless!'

'Priceless,' agreed Pointy Steve, turning his head to one side so he could see them past the bag dangling off his horn.

'I've planned this robbery down to the last detail,' Baz boasted. 'Any minute now my henchman, Lumphammer, will arrive in a submarine. It can't come right into the shore because of the rocks and things, but we'll row out to it, take the Periwinkle Cup aboard, and head for America, to begin a new life as posh millionaires!'

Max looked at the beach. Now he saw what Baz had been doing down there by the sea's edge. He had been pumping up a

little blue inflatable dinghy, which waited on the sand. And just as Max was looking at that, a dark shape broke the water far offshore. It was a submarine, and a hatch in its top popped open to reveal Baz's henchman, Lumphammer, who waved and shouted, 'Cooo-ee! Baz!'

'Excellent!' said Baz. He snatched the bag off of Pointy Steve's horn and started swaggering down the beach towards the dinghy. 'Pointy Steve!' he called over his shoulder. 'Poke that podgy pony in the wings so he can't come flapping after us!'

'Right!' said the unicorn, sounding pleased. Poking people was the part of being a unicorn that Pointy Steve liked best. (That was how he'd ended up in Horse Prison.) He lowered his head until his horn was pointing right at Kevin and said, 'Prepare for a painful poking, puny pony!'

But Kevin wasn't paying any attention. Nor was Max. Nor was Daisy. They had lost interest round about the time Baz Gumption said, 'Excellent!' Now they were all staring at the sky behind Pointy Steve's head.

A whole flock of flapping shapes had appeared there, pouring out of the woods on the sides of the island's highest mountain. They looked no bigger than a cloud of gnats at first, but then they grew closer and started to seem as if they might be the size of bats, or maybe birds. Maybe really big birds, with four legs, and tails, and . . .

'They're FLYING PONIES!' shouted Max.

'A whole flock of them!' squeaked Daisy.

'Or is it a herd?' asked Max.

'Maybe it's a flerd,' said Kevin.

'You can't fool me,' said Pointy Steve. 'You're just trying to make me look behind me so that you can run off. There aren't any ponies here.'

But there were. They came in all sorts of different sizes, from tiny foals to big old stallions, and in all sorts of different

colours—black and white, piebald and
skewbald, zebra-striped and polka-
dotted—but every one was as roly and
as poly as Kevin himself, and the whir of
their tiny wings as they dived towards the
beach was so loud that even Pointy Steve
finally looked behind him.

'Eeeeeek!' he whinnied. He forgot about
Kevin and his friends and galloped off
before the flying ponies could get him.
'Baz! Get rowing! There's LOADS of
them!' he bellowed as he thundered across
the sand towards the seashore, where
Baz was pushing the dinghy out into the

waves. Baz looked round and saw
what was happening. He jumped
into the dinghy and started
rowing as hard as he could.
Pointy Steve galloped to catch up
with him, but just as he reached
the water's edge he accidentally put
a hoof in Max's riding helmet,
which had rolled there when it fell
off Max's head.

'Ooops!' said Pointy Steve. He stumbled
and tried to stay upright and keep running,
but all four legs got tangled up. He toppled
into the waves, and his sharp horn went
straight through the side of Baz's dinghy,
which popped with a loud BANG.

'What the—?' wailed Baz, finding

himself with an oar in each hand but no boat to sit on. 'Gluggg!' he added, sinking out of sight.

A chestnut-coloured pony folded her wings and dived like a seabird into the waves. She emerged a few seconds later clutching a cross and dripping Baz by the hem of his mayoral robes. The other ponies landed all around Kevin.

'Ponies!' said Kevin. 'Roly-poly ones!'

'We didn't know there were any other flying ponies!' said Max.

'Nor did we,' said an old grey pony, coming over to nuzzle Kevin's nose. 'Hello little pony! What's your name?'

'Kevin!' said Kevin. 'I come from the wild, wet hills of the Outermost West.'

'Kevin!' the other ponies whispered. They fluttered their wings with excitement, tossed their heads, and swished their long tails about.

'I'm Colleen,' said the old grey pony. 'This is Roly-Poly Island, the home of flying ponies since the world was young. We thought we were the only ones. Have you really been nesting in the wild, wet hills of the Outermost West, all alone?'

'Well I mostly live in Bumbleford now,' said Kevin. 'And not all alone. I have Max and Daisy, and lots of other friends too. And biscuits. My favourites are Custard Creams.'

Colleen looked at Max and Daisy. 'Thank you for taking care of this pony,' she said. 'But Roly-Poly Island is where flying ponies belong.' And to Kevin she said, 'Welcome home!'

SEVEN
FLYING HOME

Kevin took a long look around. So this was his home! That explained why the island had felt so familiar, and why he had the feeling of being watched—all these ponies had been looking down at him from their nests in the high woods! Two little tears rolled down his nose, but they were tears of happiness. He had always dreamed of having other ponies to fly about with, and here they were! And

he had always said that a flying pony was meant to be a nice, round, roly-poly shape, and now he could see that he had been right!

Max took a long look too. When
the ponies appeared he had felt wildly
happy—they looked so funny and cute and
magical, tumbling through the sky. Now
that they were clustered around Kevin he
still felt happy, because he knew how much
Kevin had been wishing for some pony
friends. But he felt sad too, because he
wondered if Kevin would need his human
friends any more. Surely Kevin wouldn't
want to come back to his nest on Max's
roof. He would want to stay here with all

the other flying ponies.

And sure enough, Colleen was saying, 'We must find a tree for you to make your nest in, Kevin. There are plenty of good ones, up on the mountain there.'

But Kevin shook his head. 'I can't stay,' he said. 'Not now.'

'Why not? Why not? Of course you must!' the other ponies chorused.

'Because we have to return the Periwinkle Cup!' said Kevin. 'And catch Pointy Steve!'

But while they had been talking, Pointy Steve had swum sneakily away, climbed into the waiting submarine, and zoomed off to America with Lumphammer. It would be nice to say that they had a horrible time there, just to prove that Crime Doesn't

Pay, but actually they both did pretty well for themselves in America: Lumphammer opened quite a successful shoe shop, and Pointy Steve became President. But at least they hadn't taken the Periwinkle Cup with them—that had sunk to the bottom of the sea when Baz's boat popped.

The water wasn't very deep, so Kevin dived down and found the cup sitting on

the sea floor. There was a very proud crab standing next to it, telling an audience of shrimps and seahorses that he was delighted to accept this magnificent award, but Kevin ignored him, grabbed the cup by one of its golden handles, and swam back to shore with it.

'We have to get this cup back to the

WWHMPC,' said Max.

'And we have to get Baz Gumption back to Bumbleford Police Station,' said Daisy.

'Humph,' said Baz, who was sitting in a wet heap beside his lorry.

'But Kevin,' said Colleen, 'You've only just found your way to us! You can't leave again so soon!'

Kevin was not sure what to do. He didn't want to turn his back on all these new-found friends, but he was thinking of all his old friends at home, and also biscuits. 'I know!' he said. 'You can come too!'

So they did.

Colleen took a firm grip with her teeth on the back of Baz's trousers. Max put the Periwinkle Cup in Baz's bag and climbed onto Kevin's back with it. Of course,

Kevin couldn't be expected to carry two people and a heavy trophy, so Daisy looked around for a pony she could ride, and saw a shy little black one standing nearby, looking hopefully at her.

'Hello!' said Daisy. 'I'm Daisy, but I prefer to be called Elvira.'

'Hello!' said the black pony. 'I'm Susan, but I prefer to be called Spookarella, Pony

of the Night. I like your hair!'

'I love what you've done with your mane,' said Daisy. She had a feeling that she and Susan were going to be the best of friends. So she scrambled up on Susan's back, and, with Kevin leading the way, the whole flock, or herd, or flerd, took off and flapped across the sea towards the mainland.

There was quite a kerfuffle going on up on the top of Kerfuffle Hill. Reporters had arrived with cameras and lights to do excitable reports for the evening news, and the Bumbleford Police Force— Sergeant Gosh and PC Golightly—were going round with their notebooks, taking statements from eyewitnesses and trying to find clues. Naturally, everyone got even

more excited when the sky above the hill
suddenly filled with flying ponies.

Once they had all landed—and
the police officers had arrested Baz
Gumption—Max, Daisy, and Kevin went
to find Margery Flough. 'We found your
cup,' said Max, plonking the bag on the
grass at her feet.

'Oh, how wonderful!' said Margery
Flough, and called all the reporters over to
take photos and videos of Kevin.

'It's my Lucie's cup, actually,' snapped
Mrs Ffarthingale-Ffitch, reaching for it,
but Margery Flough brushed her away.

'Oh no it isn't, she said.

'It has come to my attention that there
may have been cheating going on during
today's race. Lucie tells me that she may
have accidentally left tripwires and muffins
on the course. That's not the sort of
attitude we encourage in the WWHMPC
at all. So I have decided that we should
run the whole race again.'

So everybody gathered to watch as the
ponies and riders took their places at the
starting line once more. Reporters and
police officers and loads of flying ponies

all stood eagerly waiting for Mrs Flough
to fire her starter's gun. It was the biggest
audience the WWHMPC had attracted
for many years. It was the biggest race for
many years, too, because when they heard
it was to be re-run, some bystanders who
had missed their chance to join in the first
time came hurrying to the starting line
alongside the unicorns. One of them was
Cedric the Centaur, who had teamed up
with his friend Doug. (Doug was a reverse
centaur, which meant he had the head of
a horse but the body and legs of a person,
and Mrs Flough agreed that the two of
them together counted as a pony and rider.)

The other new entrant was Tiffany
Binns. While everyone was waiting for
Kevin, Max, and Daisy to come back,

Tiffany had wandered down a winding
path through the woods, and come to a
little green paddock where a unicorn was
grazing. It was an odd-looking unicorn,
grey and shaggy, with long ears, and she
had known at once that it was her old
friend Bramble. They had been sitting
together near the tea tent ever since,
talking about the old days. When they
heard the race was being rerun, Tiffany

had said, 'Shall we show them
what's what?'

And Bramble had said, 'Why not!'

Max gave Tiffany her riding helmet
back. He and Kevin didn't feel like running
the race again, not after their long flight
to the island and back. So they stood with
all the other ponies, explaining the rules
to them, and leading the cheering when
the race began.

This time there was no cheating, and
whether it was because the unicorns were

tired, or because Moonshadow and the
other unicorns felt a bit sorry for being
so beastly before and deliberately went
slowly, it was Cedric and Doug who came
in second, and Tiffany Binns on Bramble
who won.

'Jolly good show!' said Margery Flough, handing Tiffany the Periwinkle Cup.

'How ridiculous!' sniffed Mrs Ffarthingale-Ffitch.

'Oh Mummy, *do* grow up,' said Lucie.

'Has anyone seen my guinea pigs?' said Ellie Fidgett, Neville and Beyoncé's owner, arriving in the middle of all the excitement. Of course everyone had seen Neville and Beyoncé—they had taken third place behind Cedric and Doug. Max's dad fetched them and handed them to Ellie, who said they were Very Naughty Guinea Pigs and kissed them on the tops of their heads. Then she put them in a fancy-looking hi-tech hutch that she had brought with her. 'I've been saving up my pocket money for this,' she explained, as she shut the door on them and typed in a combination. 'It's the PetSafe 9000, and it's guaranteed to be absolutely, positively, one hundred percent escape-proof. There's literally NO WAY Neville and Beyoncé will EVER escape again!'

(And indeed it took Neville and Beyoncé seven or eight whole minutes to find a way out.)

Later, there was tea, and squash, and biscuits, and home-made cakes, and the sun settling all comfortable and rosy-gold into the evening haze which lay above the hills. Tiffany Binns was very pleased about winning the cup, and nobody else had really minded losing, so everyone was happy.

Everyone except Max.

Max had not really been happy since
the other roly-poly ponies flew down to
save him on the island. He had been too
busy to really think about it then, and too
excited by the race to wonder much about
it afterwards, but there had been a kind of
sad feeling underneath everything since
that, and now that the prizes had been
handed out and the excitement was fading
away he started to realize what the sad

feeling was about.

Kevin did not need him any more.

All the time that Kevin had been the one-and-only roly-poly flying pony, he had needed Max as much as Max needed Kevin. They had been such good friends that they felt more like family. Max could hardly remember a time when he had not had Kevin living on his roof. He definitely couldn't imagine life without him.

But now Kevin had a real family, and friends who were as roly-poly and as flying pony-ish as himself. Why would he go on living on the roof of a tall building in Bumbleford when he could fly off across the sea and build a nest for himself among the nests of his own kind, in the trees of Roly-Poly Island?

Kevin came ambling over. Tiffany had filled the Periwinkle Cup with biscuits for him, and he had eaten them all, so he was feeling very happy, but he could see that Max wasn't. He stood next to Max, and pressed his velvety nose against Max's cheek. 'You look sad,' he said.

'I am sad,' said Max. 'I'm sad because you'll want to fly away and be with all the other flying ponies, and what will I do then? Because I need a friend, and a roly-poly flying pony is the best sort of friend.'

Then Kevin was sad too. He and Max leaned against each other for a while in a friendly, comforting sort of way while Kevin had a think. Then he twitched his ears, because he was having an idea. He thought a bit more, and decided it was a really good one. So he gave Max an encouraging nudge with his nose, and went flapping off to talk to all the other roly-poly ponies.

Daisy came over. 'What are they all talking about?' she asked Max.

'Which way to fly home, I expect,' said Max. 'I think Kevin is going to go and live on Roly- Poly Island. It is where he belongs, after all.'

'But we'll be able to visit, won't we?' asked Daisy.

'It won't be the same,' said Max

miserably. 'It will all be different. And I hate it when things change! Why can't things just stay the same?'

'Poor Max!' said Daisy, feeling sorry for him. She felt sorry for herself, too. She was going to miss Kevin, and she was going to miss Spookarella, Pony of the Night, even though they'd only just met—that little pony really understood her.

Meanwhile, Kevin kept talking to the other ponies. But he wasn't telling them how much he wanted to come and live with them on Roly-Poly Island. He was telling them about the amazing adventures he'd had since he first bumped into Max's balcony, and the brilliant friends he had made in Bumbleford, and all the interesting biscuits he had eaten.

When they had all talked it over, Kevin
spread his wings and flew back to join Max
and Daisy. 'Well,' he said, 'we have decided!'

'You're going home to live with the
other ponies, aren't you?' said Max.
'That's all right—we understand. But do
you have to go right now? Can't you stay
for one more night?'

Kevin neighed. 'Silly Max! I'm not

going to live with them! They're coming
to live with us! They really like the sound
of Bumbleford. They all want friends and
biscuits and adventures too!'

'Brilliant!' shouted Max and Daisy.

So that is why, if you ever happen to visit the little town of Bumbleford, you will see roly-poly flying ponies EVERYWHERE . . .

And, as Kevin has always said,
roly-poly flying ponies are the
best sort of flying ponies.

ABOUT THE AUTHORS

SARAH McINTYRE LIVES IN LONDON, AND PHILIP REEVE LIVES IN THE WILD WET HILLS OF DARTMOOR.

THEY MAKE UP STORIES TOGETHER, THEN PHILIP WRITES THE WORDS AND SARAH DRAWS THE PICTURES — BUT SOMETIMES SARAH HELPS PHILIP WITH THE WORDS, AND SOMETIMES PHILIP HELPS SARAH DRAW THE PICTURES.

THEY PLAN TO MAKE LOTS MORE BOOKS TOGETHER.